RUSS THOMPSON

OVERSPRAY

**Finding Forward
Books**

Published by Finding Forward Books
P.O. Box 8182, Long Beach, CA 90808
www.findingforwardbooks.com

Editing by Laura Perkins. Series concept by Pam Sheppard. Text set in Open Dyslexic Mono.

LCCN: 2021925902
ISBN: 979-8-7951488-7-8 (Amazon paperback)
ISBN: 978-1-7373157-4-2 (Ingram paperback)
FILE: FF006-25K-20250528

Summary: Ninth grader Nick Simonson is troubled and sinking fast after his dad dies in a tragic accident. His teachers don't like him, his grades are falling, and he sees no future for himself. Can he pick himself up and move forward?

BISAC Subject Codes: YOUNG ADULT FICTION / Social Themes / Emotions and Feelings | YOUNG ADULT FICTION / Social Themes / Death, Grief, and Bereavement

Lexile measure: HL520L

For Betty-Jean,
our kids,
and grandkids.

CONTENTS

1	Happen to Me	1
2	Falling	7
3	Can't Think	13
4	He Doesn't	19
5	Only Having Fun	25
6	Not Supposed	30
7	Can't Sleep	36
8	Who Cares?	40
9	Special Day	45
10	Lifted Off	51
11	Feel Bad	58
12	Long Time	63
13	Miss Him	67
14	Something Nice	71
15	Will Try	75
16	Better for Her	81
17	Proud of Me	90
18	Seven Weeks Later	96

19	Mom Smiles	101
20	Know How	104
Acknowledgments		108
About the Author		111
Finding Forward Books		112
Additional Titles		113

1 HAPPEN TO ME

MONDAY MORNING. School starts at Edison High in fifteen minutes.

Grady and I get off our skateboards and walk into Mike's Market.

Grady goes to the back to get juice. I go to the snack section to get chips.

Mr. Mike smiles when we come to the front and pay him. "Gentlemen, have a good day," he says.

We leave the store, skate two blocks, and stop.

I reach under my jacket and give Grady the chips I stole.

Grady unzips his backpack and gives me the juice he stole.

Mr. Mike is a big old guy who used to play pro football.

He looks tough on the outside. But on the inside, he's nice.

Sometimes I don't feel so good about stealing from him.

But we never steal much.

EDISON HIGH. School's out. Grady and I unlock our skateboards and walk out the front gate.

Everyone is laughing and happy.

But not me.

I got a D on my health test. I also had to serve detention at lunch because I got to school late.

"Nick, Red Church?" Grady asks.

"Sure."

We put down our boards and go.

The biggest reason I hate school,
is because I'm always at the bottom.

The other reason I hate school,
is because of the people. Everybody
acts like they're better than me.

The sidewalk is crowded with all
the happy kids walking home.

I can't stand them.

I push hard with my foot and
skate faster.

It feels good to pass them.

TEN MINUTES LATER. Grady and I turn
into the alley.

There's broken glass all over the
place, so we pick up our skateboards
and walk.

"Nick, look at that," Grady says.

It's the garage door we tagged

yesterday.

It has a fresh coat of paint. Our tagging is gone.

"Is it okay?" Grady asks.

I step back and look both ways. "Go ahead."

Grady pulls a spray can out of his backpack and tags GLIDER across the door.

I pull out my can and spray it with NEVER.

We put away our paint and start walking again.

A Conway cop car turns into the alley and comes toward us.

I get ready to run.

"Nick, be cool," Grady says. "There's no way they could have seen what we did."

The car stops next to us.

It's a young cop driving and an

old one riding.

"Gentlemen, what's up?" the old cop asks.

I try to act calm. But my heart pounds.

Grady goes to the window. "We're just going to skate."

"Where at?" the cop asks.

"The Red Church."

He looks me up and down. I get ready to run.

"That's a good place to skate," the old cop says. "See you guys later."

They drive to the end of the alley and turn left.

"Let's go," Grady says.

We walk back to the garage and bomb it again.

My dad was a Raymond cop. And my mom is a dispatcher for them.

I know I should care.
But I don't.

ALMOST DARK. We finish skating at the Red Church and walk down the alley to the back of Mike's Market.

Old Tony sits next to the trash bin. His shopping cart with everything he owns is parked next to him.

He never says anything. But he always nods, so we nod back.

I feel bad when I look at him.

Sometimes, I worry that the same thing could happen to me.

2 FALLING

HOME. I open the front door, step inside, and lock it behind me.

I always feel better when I lock the door. It feels safe, like nothing can happen to me.

One thing good about Mom working nights, is that I can do whatever I want.

But I wish she was here.

She had to start working nights about a year ago. And she doesn't usually get home until after midnight.

Sometimes I get up when she comes home, and we talk.

She tells me about her life, like how her family was poor when she was growing up, and how she always had holes in her shoes.

But when it comes to Dad, she can't talk about him.

I remember how it was when Dad would come home at night.

I would hear his footsteps come down the hall. Then he would open my door and look in on me.

It always made me feel good when he did that.

AFTER DINNER. I put my dishes in the sink, turn on the TV, and start Blaster.

The nice thing about Blaster, is that I can forget about everything

else that is happening to me. All I
have to do is play.

My phone beeps. It's a text from
Grady.

Nick, got paint?
Half can
Get more tomorrow?
Sure

The spray paint at Price Mart is
locked up.

But we know how to get it.

LATER. I sit at the kitchen table
and look at the clock on the wall.

It's after ten. I guess I'll do
some homework.

I hate English. But I like
writing in my journal because we can
say whatever we want.

Also, it's private. Mr. Rowley
doesn't read them. He just comes to
our desks and stamps the pages.
I open my notebook and begin.

Nick Simonson
English 9
Journal

*I remember back in grade school.
It was better back then.*

*Ms. Ibarra was nice. I had her
for fifth grade.*

*If you can dream it, you can
achieve it. That's what she would
tell us.*

*She always said we were special.
And I believed her.*

*Middle school was also good. The
teachers liked me. And I got mostly
A's and B's.*

But everything went bad when I got to Edison.

I try to get good grades. But now I get D's and C's.

Sometimes I just can't think. And the teachers don't like me.

Grady is my best friend. We get a lot of detentions together.

Most of the time he's cool. But sometimes he worries me because of the crazy things he does.

Stan and Carl are also cool. But I don't really know anybody else.

Mom was crying at the kitchen table when I got out of bed to see her last night.

She's a dispatcher for the Raymond Police Department.

Sometimes she hears about terrible things at her job. And she can't go to sleep when she comes home from work.

That's where she met Dad. He liked to hear her voice on the radio.

I remember the night when it happened.

He pulled a guy over for drunk driving. Dad stood next to the car.

A truck sideswiped him.

Mom was working. She heard it on the radio.

I was sleeping. Mom shook me. We rushed to the hospital and went behind the curtain.

Dad was there. But we were too late.

The life was out of him.

Mom held me.

I felt like I was falling.

3 CAN'T THINK

TUESDAY MORNING. Mom comes into the kitchen and pours a bowl of cereal.

The sleeve on her robe is frayed. I wish I could get her a new one.

"There was a kid who fell off the Raymond Street Bridge last night," she says. "He also got hit by a car. I can't stop thinking about it."

The city of Raymond is twelve miles away, so I'm sure I don't know him.

But I wonder if he was tagging. That's what worries me about

Grady.

He takes too many chances.

HEALTH. Mr. Esparza comes to the front of the classroom.

"Open your books to page 281," he says. "Read the section on tobacco. After that, I will call on you."

I begin reading. It reminds me of Uncle Terry. He smoked all the time and died of lung cancer.

That makes me think about Dad. A million cops were at his funeral.

Mom stared straight ahead. She didn't talk. All she could do was squeeze my hand.

The chief called Dad a hero. And the cops all shook our hands.

But everything else is a blur.

Ten minutes pass.

"Time's up," Mr. Esparza says.

"What are some harmful chemicals in tobacco?"

He picks a card out of his name jar. "Yesenia, could you answer?"

"Nicotine and cyanide," she says.

Mr. Esparza smiles. "Good job. What is the chemical in tobacco that causes people to get addicted?"

He pulls another card out of his name jar. "Nick, could you answer?"

I don't know what to say. My face is probably bright red.

Mr. Esparza pulls another card. "Julian, could you answer?"

I feel like an idiot. I just made myself look stupid in front of the entire class.

ENGLISH. The bell rings. Mr. Rowley comes to the front of the classroom.

"Silent reading time," he says.

"You know what to do."

The book I have is one that I pulled off the shelf when I came into the classroom.

I open to the first chapter and try to read. But the words go right by me.

I can't quit thinking about the kid who fell off the Raymond Street Bridge. It probably took just one wrong move for him to fall.

Twenty minutes pass. Mr. Rowley comes to the front of the classroom.

"Francine, what are you reading?" he asks.

"It's about a family. They're always arguing and fussing at each other. The main character is a girl in high school."

"Very good," Mr. Rowley says. "Nick, what about your book?"

It's my second time being called on in the same day. I have to think fast. I didn't read any of it.

"It's about a guy who has to leave his family," I say. "I'm at the beginning, where he says goodbye to them."

"What's the name of the book?"

"*The Long Goodbye*."

"Interesting," Mr. Rowley says.

I hope I'm not caught.

Ten minutes pass. We're supposed to be writing papers about the story we read yesterday.

I try to write. But I keep thinking about the kid who fell.

Mr. Rowley comes to my desk and kneels next to me. "Nick, can I see your book?"

I don't want to show it to him. But I have no choice.

He skims the first pages and frowns. "I can tell from what you said that you didn't read this. What's going on?"

"I don't know. Sometimes I see the words. But I just can't think."

4 HE DOESN'T

TUESDAY. After school. Grady and I get to Price Mart.

I don't like what we're going to do. But with Grady, I always follow along.

The shelf rack with the spray paint has a locked metal screen in front of it. But there's no screen behind it.

We go to the row behind the spray paint.

Grady looks both ways. "Nick, it's clear."

I crawl under the shelf rack, grab two cans of black, and crawl out.

I give them to Grady. He smiles.

I go back for two more cans and crawl out again.

We put the paint in the linings of our jackets, split up, and meet at the hardware section.

The gloves we use for tagging are the cloth kind. I grab a two-pack for $3.99.

We go to the front and pay for the gloves.

The lady at the cash register looks at me like she suspects something.

I look away.

We walk out the door and don't look back.

"It's funny," Grady says.

"Stealing the paint is almost the
same rush as tagging with it."

It's a rush for him. But it's
scary for me.

LATER. Grady and I carry our
skateboards and walk through the
alley behind the Red Church.

Stan and Carl walk ahead of us.
They're skaters. But they don't tag.

I see the garage door from
yesterday.

"Looks like the old man painted
over our tags again," Grady says.
"We'll have to come back tonight."

I look up and see a new spy
camera under the roof eave. "Grady,
do you see that?"

"No problem," he says. "I know
what to do."

We go through the back gate of

the church and begin skating.

Grady, Carl, and Stan do stair
tricks down the back steps.

I stick to ground tricks and fall
on my elbow when I try to do a
kickflip.

It's the second time I've fallen
on my elbow this week.

This time, it's worse.

TEN-THIRTY. The alley is dark. Grady
and I get to the garage door that
was painted over.

Everything is quiet.

We put on our gloves and pull out
our spray cans.

"Watch this," Grady says.

He climbs on top of the block
wall next to the garage and sprays
the lens of the spy camera.

He steps sideways and smiles down

at me. It's like a game to him.

A brick under his foot comes loose.

He falls sideways into the backyard.

Thunk.

"Grady, are you okay?" I whisper.

No sound.

"Grady?"

He must be hurt. I grab the top of the wall and try to pull myself up.

But I can't because of my elbow.

"Grady, can you hear me?"

No sound.

A door opens. I hear running.

A man's voice calls out. "Alice, call the paramedics!"

His voice gets softer. "Don't worry, son. Hang on."

Minutes pass. I hear sirens.

Grady is my best friend. He has to be okay.

A police car and paramedics come up the alley with their red lights flashing.

I hide behind some trash cans.

The back gate opens.

I hear the old man's voice. "He's right here."

The paramedics go in the gate. I can't see what's happening.

I hear voices. More time passes.

They wheel Grady out on a stretcher and put him into the back of the paramedic van.

I watch for him to move.

But he doesn't.

5   ONLY HAVING FUN

WEDNESDAY. Lunch. Stan and Carl are already at our table when I get there.

Carl takes a bite out of his sandwich. "Nick, have you seen Grady today?"

I don't want to talk about what happened last night. Maybe Grady will be okay.

"Not at all," I say. "Maybe he decided to ditch."

"Are you going to skate after school?" Stan asks.

"Not sure. I might have some
other stuff to do."

The sound comes back to me from
when Grady fell.

Thunk.

I wonder if it was his head
hitting something.

I kept hoping he would move when
the paramedics put him into their
van.

I close my eyes and hear the
thunk again.

ENGLISH. Grady's desk is empty. I
can't stop thinking about him.

There's a knock on the door.

Ms. Boyle, a counselor, comes
into the classroom. She whispers
into Mr. Rowley's ear.

His face turns gray.

A message comes over the

intercom. "This is Dr. Vinson, the principal. I regret to report a tragic accident involving one of our students. Grady Linsky, a ninth grader, received a serious head injury in a fall last night. I'm sorry to say the doctors were unable to save him. He passed away this morning."

The classroom goes silent.

The principal says more. But I don't hear any of it.

Grady was my best friend.

He's gone.

TEN-THIRTY. I open the front door and step outside.

It's darker than usual. There's no moon tonight.

I shut the door, lock it, and walk down the back steps to the alley.

A dog barks from behind a fence.
I don't care.

More dogs bark. I still don't
care.

I pull up my hoodie and keep
walking.

Ten minutes later, I'm at the
garage where Grady fell.

I put on my gloves, take out my
spray can, and paint NEVER across
the front of it.

A light comes on from the back
porch.

A door opens.

I run.

HOME. I step inside and lock the
door behind me.

I'm safe. But I don't feel
better.

I remember Grady's laugh.
I wish I could hear it again.
We were only having fun.

6 NOT SUPPOSED

THURSDAY MORNING. Breakfast. I sit at the kitchen table and look at the toaster again.

I need to put bread in it. But I can't get up. All I can do is stare.

Mom comes into the kitchen and sits across from me. "Nick, what's wrong?"

I don't say anything.

"What's wrong?" she asks again.

I don't want to talk. But I can't hold it in.

"There was an accident," I say.

"Grady died."

Silence.

She reaches across the table to hold my hand. "What happened?"

I look down. I don't want her to see the tears in my eyes. "The principal made an announcement yesterday. Grady fell and died. He had a head injury."

"How did he fall?"

"I don't know."

I wish I could tell her the truth. But I wasn't supposed to be there.

I'm glad when she squeezes my hand.

AFTER BREAKFAST. I skate down the sidewalk to school.

The sky is gray.

The sidewalk is gray.

Everything is gray.

Grady should be skating next to me.

But he's gone.

Mike's Market is the first stop. I grab a bag of chips and go to the front.

"Where's Grady?" Mr. Mike asks.

"He had a fall."

"Tell him I hope he feels better."

I go outside and get on my skateboard.

The tears start. I wipe them away. There's no way I can go to school today.

I turn the corner and step into the alley. Old Tony sits next to the trash bin.

He coughs. It comes from deep inside him, like he's really sick.

I walk two more blocks to the
garage where Grady died.

It still has my tag on it, NEVER.

I sit at the spot where I hid
last night.

The wall has a missing brick now.

Grady is gone.

THREE-THIRTY. I get to Grady's
apartment and knock on the door.

His mom answers. Her eyes are
red, like she's been crying. "Nick,
I was hoping you would come."

I sit with her in the living
room. She gives me a notebook. It's
Grady's tagging book.

"Do you know what this is?" she
asks.

"No."

"It has writing in it," she says.
"The same stuff I see on the walls

around here. I also found a can of
spray paint."

She looks like she might cry
again. "Were you tagging with him?"

"No."

"Did you know he was tagging?"

"No."

"Were you with him when it
happened?"

"No."

I feel bad about lying. But I
don't want to get in trouble for
being there.

HOME. I open the front door and step
inside.

I don't know why, but I don't
feel safe when I lock it.

Then I see it, on top of the
kitchen table.

It's my tagging book and spray

cans.

Mom searched my room.

I'm caught.

I think of Grady, and how he smiled before he fell.

It was not supposed to be this way.

7 CAN'T SLEEP

I LIE IN BED. My mind won't stop. I look at the alarm clock. It's after midnight.

The front door opens. Mom comes in. I listen as her steps come down the hall.

She opens my door and turns on the light. "Nick, we need to talk."

I have to be convincing. I rub my eyes and act like I was sleeping.

"Why did I find that stuff in your room?" she asks.

"It wasn't mine. It was Grady's."

"What are you talking about?"

"He was keeping it here so his mom wouldn't find it."

"What about when he fell? Was he tagging?"

"He might have been," I say. "He would go out by himself at night and tell me about it the next day."

"Why weren't you in school today?"

"What do you mean?"

"I got a text message from the attendance office. It said you were absent from all your classes."

"It wasn't me. It was probably some kind of mix-up."

"You're right," Mom says. "Something is mixed up. Come with me."

I follow her to the kitchen. She opens the laptop and gets on School

View.

"I'm sorry about Grady," she says. "And I know it's been hard for you with Dad gone. But you haven't done any homework for the last three weeks."

"Yes, I have. The teachers just haven't checked it yet."

"Interesting," she says. "I guess it's another mix-up."

I know she doesn't believe me. I've always been able to fool her before.

BACK IN BED. I listen as Mom moves around in the kitchen.

Grady's face comes back to me. He stood on the wall, smiled, and was gone.

Next, I see Dad in my mind. He left for work, got hit by a truck, and was gone.

    I look at my alarm clock. It's
one in the morning.

    I can't sleep.

8 WHO CARES?

FRIDAY MORNING. Mom pulls into the parking lot of Edison High School.

"Please Mom," I say. "We don't need to do this."

"Yes, we do," she says. "This nonsense with your grades is going to stop."

We walk through the front gate and go toward the counseling office.

Everyone is looking at me.

I wish I could melt into the floor.

COUNSELING OFFICE. We sit in the waiting area. Ms. Boyle comes out and waves for us to come into her office.

I stand to go in.

"Wait here," Mom says. "This is going to be between your counselor and me."

Mom goes inside. Ms. Boyle closes the door.

I wish I knew what they were saying.

TWENTY MINUTES LATER. Ms. Boyle comes out and waves for me to come into her office.

Mom's eyes are red. She's been crying.

I feel bad about what she's going through. I wish I could make her happy again.

"Nick, I know that things have been hard for you," Ms. Boyle says. "But the reality, is that you have to change. You have two D's and two NoPasses on your report card. There's no excuse for it."

I look out the window. It doesn't help.

"The choices you make now are going to affect you the rest of your life," Ms. Boyle says. "If you don't start applying yourself, things are going to get much worse for you."

I already know that.

It's already happening.

Everything is falling apart.

LUNCH. I walk to the food court and get in line.

Everyone seems so happy. But not me.

I see a short guy with a black hoodie up ahead.

It's Grady!

He turns around. It's not.

It's the second time today this has happened to me. I can't get him out of my mind.

I get to our table. Stan and Carl are already there.

"Where were you yesterday?" Carl asks.

"I ditched."

"What for?"

How can he ask such a stupid question?

ENGLISH. Mr. Rowley stands at the door. I walk to my seat and say nothing.

Grady's empty desk is next to me. I try not to look at it.

Mr. Rowley comes to the front of the classroom. "Your test tomorrow is on..."

I look at Grady's desk again.

Who cares?

9 SPECIAL DAY

AFTER SCHOOL. I leave out the front
gate. Everybody else is happy.

But not me.

Two days ago, I was skating home
with Grady.

Never again.

ALMOST HOME. I stop at Mike's
Market, grab a bag of chips, and go
to the back to get a soda.

I see Grady in my mind. He's
smiling and laughing, like he was
never gone. I think about what he

would do if he was here.

I put away the soda, grab two beers, and hide them inside my jacket.

Mr. Mike stands at the counter when I pay for the chips.

"I'm sorry about Grady," he says. "I know you guys were friends."

I keep my eyes down. If I look at Mr. Mike, I might lose it.

"Did you give a card to his mom?" he asks.

"I never thought of it."

"Go to the back, get one, and take it to her. It's on me."

I go to the back and find a card.

The beer cans feel heavy as I walk out the door.

I don't feel good about stealing from Mr. Mike today.

ALLEY. I get to the spot where Grady died.

My tag on the garage door has been painted over. The loose brick has been fixed.

It's like we were never there.

I sit down, open the first can of beer, and begin sipping.

The taste is okay now. But I've never been able to gulp it like Grady could.

I look around the alley. It's nice to be alone.

The next can of beer tastes better. I like the way it slows my brain down.

I wish Dad was here.

Saturday mornings were good. He would take me running with him. We would always stop somewhere and talk about things.

I wish I could go running with him now.

My phone buzzes. It's a text from Mom.

Nick, where are you?

Skating

Where?

Red church

Get home now

I finish the rest of the beer and stand up. I'm a little wobbly.

Then, I remember. My skateboard is at home because Mom took me to school this morning.

HOME. I get to the front door and wait before I open it.

I know what I have to say. But I have to say it right, so Mom will believe me.

And I have to breathe lightly, so she won't smell the beer on my breath.

She's sitting on the couch when I get inside. My skateboard lies on the floor next to her.

"My supervisor gave me the night off," she says. "I was worried because you weren't here."

I step to the easy chair. My foot catches on the carpet. I almost fall.

"What have you been drinking?" she asks.

"Nothing."

Her face turns red. "Why does it smell like you were?"

"I don't know."

"You said you were skating. How were you doing it without a

skateboard?"

"I was using Stan's."

"Were Stan and Carl drinking too?"

"None of us were drinking."

Her face gets hard. "I know you've been drinking. And you're lying to me. That makes it worse."

I look away from her. I wish I was back in the alley.

Her eyes drill into me. "I'm glad tomorrow is Saturday. We're going to have a special day together."

10 LIFTED OFF

SATURDAY MORNING. I want to keep
sleeping. But the sun shines in my
eyes.

Dad's face comes back to me. I
remember his funeral.

I tried to be strong for Mom. But
I lost it and started crying in
front of all those cops.

Six months later, and it's still
not any better.

My door opens. Mom comes in.

"Are you ready?" she asks.

"For what?"

"Things are going to change," she
says. "We're going for a run."

AFTER BREAKFAST. Mom and I step
outside. The sun feels nice on my
face.

We walk down the stairs, go out
the front gate, and begin running.

Mom is not very fast. I go slow,
so she can stay with me.

That's how it was with Dad. He
would go slow, so I could stay with
him.

We reach Edison and run along the
path that goes around the baseball
field.

Mom slows down. We get to the
bleachers.

"Let's take a rest," I say.

It's one of the places where Dad
and I used to stop.

We sit down. Mom's face has a
soft look to it, like she's not mad
at me anymore.

"What really happened yesterday?"
she asks.

I don't want to tell her. But I'm
tired of lying. "I took beer from
Mike's Market."

Silence.

"How did you do that?" she asks.

"I put it in the lining of my
jacket."

"How long have you been
drinking?"

"Not very long. I would do it
with the guys. But it wasn't out of
control or anything."

It's not true. We used to get
blasted.

But I can't tell her everything.

AFTER LUNCH. Mom and I walk up the stairs to Grady's apartment.

I wish she wasn't with me. But I don't have a choice.

I ring the bell. Ms. Linsky opens the door.

I try to say something. But nothing comes out. I give Ms. Linsky the sympathy card.

Mom steps forward and hugs her.

Somehow, I feel better.

We sit on the couch in the living room. I see Grady's tagging book on the coffee table.

I hope Mom doesn't notice it.

Ms. Linsky wipes her eyes. "The police said it happened when Grady was tagging. He fell off a wall and hit his head on a brick walkway."

"I'm so sorry," Mom says. "I really liked Grady. He was always a gentleman when he came by."

They continue talking. Ms. Linsky smiles. I'm glad Mom came with me.

LATER. Mom and I get home. She has a look on her face like I'm in trouble again.

"I saw the tagging book on the coffee table," she says. "Did Grady have two of them?"

"No," I say. "The book you found at our house was mine."

I explain about everything, the tagging, the stealing, and the night Grady died.

I didn't want to tell her. But I feel better now.

The lying is over.

AFTERNOON. Mom and I step into Mike's Market.

He stands behind the counter and
smiles when we come inside.

Mom looks at me and taps my arm.
But I can't talk.

"Mr. Mike," Mom says. "Nick has
something to say to you."

It's hard to face him. But I have
to do it.

I explain how I stole the beer. I
also tell how Grady and I would
steal chips and juice every morning.

I feel drained when I finish.

"Why did you do it?" Mr. Mike
asks. "I thought we were friends."

I figured he would be mad. But
this is worse.

"Nick thought it would be good if
he worked off what he stole," Mom
says. "He could come every day after
school."

"I like that," Mr. Mike says. "I

can also use the help."

I feel better when we leave the store.

It's like a weight has been lifted off my shoulders.

11 FEEL BAD

MONDAY AFTERNOON. I get to Mike's
Market and go in the front door.

I didn't think I would be
nervous. But I am.

Mr. Mike stands behind the
counter. Ms. Kacie, his wife, stands
next to him.

I feel better when they smile.

"Nick, are you ready to start?"
Mr. Mike asks.

"Yep, I'm ready."

He takes me to the storage room.
It's filled with boxes of stuff for

the store shelves.

"I'm going to need you to do stocking every day," Mr. Mike says. "You take items from the boxes in here and fill up the shelves in the store."

"Okay."

"I also need you to help with the inventory," he says. "It's where you count everything in the store. I'll show you after you finish stocking the shelves."

He gives me a green store vest and puts his hand on my shoulder.

"I'm glad you're working here," he says. "I think you're going to learn some things."

It feels good to put on the store vest. It makes me feel like I belong to something.

TWO HOURS LATER. I finish stocking the shelves. Mr. Mike comes into the storage room and sits across from me.

"I thought about how you were stealing beer," he says. "I did the same thing when I was in high school. I was with some buddies from the football team. We were too young to buy it, so we stole it."

"What happened?"

"The store owner caught us and told our football coach. We got in big trouble."

I try to picture Mr. Mike playing football. He seems so old now.

"What was it like in the pros?" I ask.

"It had always been my dream to play," he says. "But I wrecked it by being stupid."

"What happened?"

"It was my fourth season. I was drunk at a party and cut my arm when I shoved it through a window. I injured the nerves and lost the strength in my arm. After that, I had to retire."

"How old were you?"

"I was only twenty-six," he says. "That was thirty years ago. I kept drinking, and things got worse. Luckily, I met Kacie. She's the one who saved me."

He stands. I notice how his left arm is skinnier than his right arm.

"It's your life," he says. "Think hard about what you do. If you make good decisions, it will help you. If you make bad ones, it will mess you up."

AFTER WORK. I leave Mike's Market
from the back door and walk by Old
Tony.

We nod to each other like we
always do. But we don't say
anything.

He coughs. It sounds worse than
it was the other day.

It begins to rain. I watch as he
covers himself up with a sheet of
plastic.

I feel bad for him.

12 LONG TIME

TUESDAY MORNING. School starts in thirty minutes. I leave our apartment and go out the back gate to the alley.

First, I pass the spot where Grady died. I keep my eyes straight ahead and try not to look there.

Next, I get to Old Tony's spot. It's not raining anymore. But he's still covered up with his plastic sheet.

I can't see him. But I can hear him cough.

I put a bag down next to him with some stuff I brought from home.

It has a blanket, a jacket, and a sandwich I made.

I hope it helps.

AFTER SCHOOL. Mike's Market. I stock chips in the snack section. It feels good to see the shelves get full.

Stan and Carl come in. They don't notice me and go to the back where the drinks are.

I think I know what they're going to do. I move to the next row where I can watch them.

Stan slides open the glass door where the beer is. Carl reaches in to grab one.

"Really?" I ask.

They turn around, give me a surprised look, and grab sodas.

I never would have said anything
before. But Mr. Mike is trying to
help me.

I'm glad they don't seem mad.

HOME. I finish my homework. Mom
works tonight. Everything is quiet.

I get on the laptop and look up
Mr. Mike. He played four years with
the New York Giants and was the
youngest lineman to make the Pro
Bowl.

I knew he was good. But I didn't
know he was great. He acts like just
a regular guy.

MIDNIGHT. I should be sleeping. But
I can't get my brain to shut off.

The front door opens. Mom comes
down the hallway and looks into my
room.

"Hi Mom," I say.

She turns on the light. "Nick, guess what happened. I got a thank-you letter about Dad."

"What do you mean?"

"A lady wrote to the police department a long time ago to say thank you. She got into a crash and her car was burning. Dad pulled her out and saved her life."

I remember the last time I saw Dad. It was breakfast. I never saw him again.

Then it happens. I feel tears coming.

Mom holds me for a long time.

13 MISS HIM

WEDNESDAY MORNING. School starts in thirty minutes.

I walk down the alley behind Mike's Market. Old Tony is there under his plastic sheet.

I'm glad I don't hear him coughing. I was worried about him when it was raining last night.

The sun is out now. I'm glad it will be dry for him today.

ENGLISH. Mr. Rowley hands back our tests from yesterday.

Mine is a C. I smile to myself.
My other classes today were also
good.

Mr. Mike was right. It feels good
to be studying and doing my homework
now.

AFTER SCHOOL. There's a police car
and people standing around when I
get to the alley behind Mike's
Market.

Mr. Mike stands off to the side.
He has a look on his face like
something is very wrong.

I wonder if he got robbed.

"What happened?" I ask.

"It's Old Tony," he says. "I came
out this afternoon to check on
things. The sandwich I put next to
him this morning was still there. He
didn't answer, so I bent down to

68

shake him. He was cold and stiff
when I touched him."

The breath goes out of me. Mr.
Mike has tears in his eyes.

I wonder if Old Tony was dead
when I passed him this morning.

LATER. I leave the apartment and
walk down the stairs. It's going to
be hard working for Mr. Mike today.

I step inside the market. It's
busy and people are buying things.

But it's quiet.

I go to the storage room and put
on my store vest.

Mr. Mike comes in. "Nick, are you
okay?"

I think about Dad. I think about
Grady and Old Tony. All of them are
gone.

"Do you think I could do

something for Old Tony?" I ask.

"Like what?"

"Would it be okay if I painted something on your back wall, something in his memory?"

He smiles and puts his hand on my shoulder. "I like that. I'll go down and get some spray paint."

HOME. I walk in the front door. It's been a sad day.

I painted REST IN PEACE, OLD TONY, on the back wall of the market. Mr. Mike said he was proud of me for doing it.

I close my eyes and think about Old Tony.

I didn't know him. But I'm going to miss him.

14 SOMETHING NICE

THURSDAY. Lunch. I reach the food court and get in line. Everything is crowded and busy.

I see our table. Stan and Carl are already there. It's hard to look at the spot where Grady would sit.

On the outside, Grady seemed happy. He was always joking around and laughing.

But on the inside, he was hurting.

It bugged him that he was bad in school. And it bugged him that he had never known his dad.

He tried to cover it up. But we would talk. I knew what he was going through.

Two girls stand in line in front of me. I don't know them.

"Did you hear about the kid who died?" the first one asks.

"The one from last week?"

"I heard he was a tagger," the first one says. "He was tagging when he fell."

"Do you remember his name?"

"No. He was a nobody."

I leave the food line, go to the PE yard, and sit on the bleachers where it's empty.

Grady was not a nobody.

SEVEN O'CLOCK. I leave Mike's Market, get on my skateboard, and go to Price Mart.

I reach the paint section, crawl
behind the shelf, and grab two cans
of black.

I'm nervous when I leave the
store. But I'm doing it for Grady.

TEN O'CLOCK. I stand on the sidewalk
behind Edison High School and pull
up my hoodie.

The streetlight is burned out.
That's good. Nobody will see me.

I step to the spot where the
fence is loose, pull up the bottom,
and crawl under.

I'm going to show those girls who
Grady was.

The first building I reach is the
gym. I spray it with Grady's tag,
GLIDER.

I also tag GLIDER on the main

building and the library.

Grady would smile if he could see me.

Next, I go to the science building. The metal ball inside the spray can clicks when I shake it.

A door opens. I hide behind some bushes.

A custodian comes out and looks in my direction. But he doesn't see me and goes back inside.

I go around to the rest of the school and empty my second can of spray paint.

It feels good to do something nice for Grady.

15 WILL TRY

FRIDAY MORNING. I can't wait to see
Grady's tags at school.

But when I get there, they've all
been painted over.

It's like I was never there.

HEALTH. Mr. Esparza comes to the
front of the classroom.

"Who can tell me what depression
is?" he asks.

A girl raises her hand. "It's
when everything is going bad. You
feel down, like you'll never come

out of it."

"Think about your own life," he says. "How many of you know someone who could be suffering from depression?"

About half the kids raise their hands. I wonder if that's what is happening to me.

There's a knock on the door. It's a blue slip for me to go to the dean's office.

I get a bad feeling.

DEANS' OFFICE. I sit across the desk from Mr. Wiley.

I try to act calm. But I shake inside.

"I saw an interesting video this morning," he says. "Who is GLIDER?"

I don't say anything. What proof could he have?

He shows me his computer screen. There I am, painting GLIDER on the main building.

Then, it shows my face. I looked right at the camera.

"The principal saw your tags early this morning," Mr. Wiley says. "He called in two extra custodians to paint over everything before school started. What were you thinking?"

I don't know what to say.

He dials his phone. "Hello, Ms. Simonson?... This is Mr. Wiley from Edison High School... It's about Nick. We have him on video... He was tagging the school last night... Thanks. See you soon."

Mom doesn't deserve this. I feel awful.

THIRTY MINUTES LATER. Mom and I sit together in Mr. Wiley's office.

Her eyes are red, like she was crying before she got here.

"How much was the damage?" she asks Mr. Wiley.

"Between the paint costs and the man-hours, about seven hundred dollars."

Mom looks at me like she's going to cry again.

Mr. Wiley asks me to sit outside in the waiting area.

What have I done?

Ten minutes pass. Mr. Wiley comes out and waves me back into his office.

"You're going to pay for what you did by doing a month of school beautification," he says. "You're also going to do in-school suspension."

I feel relieved that we don't
have to pay any money.

But a month of school
beautification is a long time.

IN-SCHOOL SUSPENSION. I go straight
to the guidance room from Mr.
Wiley's office.

The lady in charge shows me where
to sit. I have to write about what I
did wrong and how I will improve in
school.

Nick Simonson
In-School Suspension

*I got sent here for tagging on
the walls last night. I shouldn't
have done it.*

But I was mad because my friend

died.

His name was Grady Linsky. I wanted people to remember him.

I used to like school. But everything about it has been bad this year.

No matter what I do, it keeps getting worse and worse.

I can do the work. But I always end up thinking about other things.

With Dad gone, and now Grady, everything is bad.

I apologize for painting on the walls last night.

I know it was wrong. I will try to make things better.

16 BETTER FOR HER

AFTER SCHOOL. I get to the custodial shop.

I don't want to be here. But I don't have a choice after what I did last night.

Mr. Damon comes to the front, wheeling his cleaning cart. "Are you Nick?"

"Yep."

"Good," he says. "You take the cart."

I pretend not to hear him. I don't want to push it with the other kids watching.

"I know you don't want to," Mr.
Damon says. "But it's part of your
job."

I take the cart and begin
pushing.

Mr. Damon walks next to me as we
go to the math building.

He's an old guy who moves like
his back is stiff. I wonder how long
he's been working here.

"I've seen you around," Mr. Damon
says. "Why did you do it?"

My face gets hot. "I don't know.
It just happened."

I'm surprised when he doesn't say
anything more. I'm also glad.

We get to the first classroom.

"I take this job seriously," Mr.
Damon says. "Every classroom we
clean has to be done right."

He shows me how to empty the pencil sharpener and dump the trash.

I have to do it perfectly, just like he says.

The last job is cleaning the floor. He shows me how to get around the chair legs with the dust mop.

I finish. But he finds dirt and makes me clean the floor again.

"Not bad," he finally says. "You're doing better than I thought you would."

I didn't expect him to say that.

It makes me want to work harder for him.

SECOND ROOM. Mr. Damon unlocks the door and sits in the back.

"You know what to do," he says. "This one is all yours."

It's Mr. Braden's room. He always

makes us keep things clean. But I
guess there was a sub today.

There are paper balls, chip bags,
and a dripping soda can on the
floor.

Now that I have to clean, it
makes me mad to see things messed
up.

I get to work.

"Did you have fun tagging the
school last night?" Mr. Damon asks.

"Not really."

"Do you think it was fun for the
people who had to paint over it?"

"No."

"Why did you do it?"

I don't want to answer. He
wouldn't understand. But I have to
say something.

"I was doing it for my friend," I
say. "He died. A girl said he was a

nobody."

"What does tagging the school
have to do with your friend?"

"That's what he used to do. But
he got killed doing it."

"Was that Grady Linsky, the boy
who fell?"

"Yep, that was him."

I feel tears coming. I turn away
from Mr. Damon and start on the
floor.

"I'm sorry about your friend," he
says.

I keep working. I'm glad Mr.
Damon doesn't ask any more
questions.

ANOTHER CLASSROOM. Mr. Damon sits in
the back again. I empty the trash
and begin scraping gum off the
floor.

"How was tagging the school going to help your friend?" Mr. Damon asks.

"I just wanted to do something to remember him by."

"Is there more?"

I'm not sure if I should tell him. But he seems like he cares.

"My dad died six months ago," I say. "He was a police officer. He pulled a guy over for drunk driving, and a truck hit him. Another man I know died two days ago. His name was Old Tony."

Silence.

"I'm sorry for your losses," Mr. Damon says. "You've been through some terrible times."

Tears start to come. I look away and hold them back.

"No matter how bad things may

get, always remember that you have
your future in front of you," Mr.
Damon says.

"What do you mean?"

"You can't do anything about the
bad things that have already
happened. But you can move forward
and make the most of what you have."

"How do I do that?"

"Think about your dad. What can
you do to make him proud of you?
Think about your mom. Is there
something you can do to make things
easier for her?"

We go to the next classroom and
the next, always talking.

I didn't think I would like
cleaning classrooms. But I do.

And it's not so bad pushing the
cart.

EVENING. Mom and I get to Burger House.

I'm glad we still come on Fridays. But I wish Dad was with us. I remember how he would listen to me.

We place our orders and find a table by the front window.

"How was cleaning today?" Mom asks.

"I worked with Mr. Damon. We talked about a lot of stuff. It wasn't as bad as I thought it would be."

She reaches across the table to hold my hand. "I remember Mr. Damon from when I went to Edison. Sometimes, he would talk to us while he worked. He cared about the school and tried to help us. Your dad was like that. He cared about people.

And he cared about doing a good
job."

I look in her eyes and see the
pain she's going through.

I feel bad about what I've done.
I hope I can make things better for
her.

17 PROUD OF ME

SATURDAY MORNING. I step into the alley where Grady died. It seems strange to be carrying a push broom.

But I think about what Mr. Damon said, about making things right.

The broken glass has been here for a long time. I start at the end of the alley and begin sweeping.

The more I clean, the better I feel.

I reach the garage door where Grady fell. It's been tagged again.

I think about the old people who

live there. They tried to help
Grady.

I know it will be hard. But I
have to do it.

I walk around to the street side
of the house and go to the front
door.

I ring the bell. An old lady
answers. It surprises me when she
smiles.

I try not to let my voice shake.
"My name is Nick. I want to
apologize for what I did."

"What was that?" she asks.

"I put spray paint on your garage
door a couple weeks ago. I'm the one
who tagged it with NEVER."

A wrinkled old man wearing
farmer's overalls comes up and
stands next to her.

He looks me in the eye and shakes

my hand.

"Come in," he says. "We're glad
to meet you."

I follow them into the kitchen.
Their names are Mr. and Ms. Pollard.
They've lived in the house for
fifty-three years.

I tell them what happened on the
night when Grady died.

"I'm sorry about your friend,"
Ms. Pollard says. She has a tear in
her eye.

"It was a terrible night," says
Mr. Pollard. "I will never forget
it."

"I was wondering if I could help
you," I say.

"What would that be?" he asks.

"I already swept your alley. I
was wondering if I could paint over
the tagging on your garage door. I

could also do it for your
neighbors."

Both of them smile.

"Thank you," Mr. Pollard says.
"That would be a big help to us."

I feel good about myself as I
paint their garage door.

Dad would smile if he could see
me.

PRICE MART. I go to customer
service. It's hard not to be
nervous.

I tell the man what I want to do.
He calls for the assistant manager.

She's a thin lady with gray hair.
Her Price Mart vest is faded, like
she's worked here for a long time.

"Can I help you?" she asks.

My voice shakes as I tell her
about the paint we stole.

I show her how I would crawl under the shelf racks. I even tell her how Grady died.

I expect her to be mad. But her eyes are kind.

"What you're doing is very brave, she says. "It takes a lot of courage to admit what you did."

I reach into my pocket and pull out the seventy-eight dollars I brought. It took a long time to save it.

"This is to pay for the paint we took. I apologize for what we did."

She accepts the money and shakes my hand.

Dad would be proud of me.

TEN-THIRTY. I sit at the kitchen table with my laptop.

I finished my work in health and

history. All I have left is math.

It seems strange to be doing homework on a Saturday night. But Mr. Damon was right about what I need to do.

I feel good about what I'm doing.

I'm going to make Mom proud of me.

18   SEVEN WEEKS LATER

SATURDAY MORNING. Mike's Market. The shelves are stocked now. I take a break in the storage room.

Mr. Mike comes in. "I had to go through a lot of red tape with Vernon County and the Department of Veterans Affairs. But I finally got things set up for Old Tony's funeral. Did you ask your mom if you could go?"

"She said it's okay. And she's coming too. She wants to pay her respects."

Mr. Mike smiles.

"Did you know Old Tony very well?" I ask.

"We talked every day. He was a smart guy. But he had a lot of problems."

"How come he didn't have a home?"

"When he got out of the Army, his head was messed up. Every time he got a job, he would get mad about something, start drinking, and get fired. He didn't have a family to fall back on."

I think about Old Tony on the day before he died. "I wish I had done more than nod to him each day. I gave him a jacket and a blanket. But it was too late."

"It's never too late," Mr. Mike says. "You showed him you cared, and I'm sure he knew that. Some people

could have thought it was too late
for you, too. But look what happened
when you decided to change."

I've been working hard in my
classes, and my grades are much
better now.

For the first time since Dad
died, I feel good about myself.

AFTERNOON. Stan and Carl are in the
alley with me. We finish painting
the last garage door.

"Did you ever think you would be
a reverse tagger?" Carl asks me.

"No way. But I like it."

The gate opens from Mr. Pollard's
yard. He comes into the alley with
cash in his hand.

"The rest of the neighbors also
pitched in," he says. "Thanks for
the job you guys are doing."

He counts off fifteen dollars for
each of us. It's a good feeling to
get paid.

I look again at the sign Mr.
Pollard painted on his wall. It
says, REST IN PEACE, GRADY.

He did it carefully with a brush.
The lettering looks like it was done
by an artist.

I feel sad when I look at the
sign. But I'm glad that Grady is
being remembered.

PRICE MART. I push the cart and
follow Mom. We go to the food
section.

Now that I'm not stealing, I feel
good about being here.

A lady comes up to us and smiles.
It's the assistant manager.

"Are you Ms. Simonson?" she asks.

"Yes. Can I help you?"

"I wanted to say thanks," she says. "Nick came to me and paid for the spray paint he took. I will never forget it."

"I'm sorry about what happened," Mom says.

"When he admitted what he did, it showed a lot," the assistant manager says. "If he needs a job when he turns sixteen, I know we could use him."

Mom smiles and puts her hand on my shoulder.

I remember what Mr. Mike said about making good decisions.

I know what he means now.

19 MOM SMILES

SUNDAY AFTERNOON. Cemetery. Mom and I sit on the grass in front of Dad's grave.

The trees and flowers make me feel peaceful inside.

Mom holds my hand. "Every time we come here, I feel like Dad is with us."

"Me too," I say. "But I wish he could be with us for real."

Mom squeezes my hand. "Dad told me he only wanted one thing for you. He wanted you to be a good person. I know he would be proud of you."

I look at the sky and think about how hard things have been. "I know I was messing up. It felt like I was sinking lower and lower."

"You've been through a lot," Mom says. "But you're making it now."

I touch Dad's grave marker. It says, JOHN SIMONSON, HUSBAND AND FATHER.

Mom looks at me. "Are you ready?"

I take out the hand shovel I brought and slice into the grass.

Mom puts in her letter. I put in mine. It makes me feel close to Dad when I push the grass down.

We walk to the car. Mom holds my hand.

"What did you write?" she asks.

"I told him about all the things I did wrong, and how I'm doing better now."

"That must have been a lot of pages."

Mom smiles at me. It feels good to laugh.

20 KNOW HOW

MONDAY MORNING. School starts in thirty minutes.

I pick up my skateboard and walk through the door of Mike's Market.

I go to the back, get a package of notebook paper, and bring it to the front.

"Nick, good job again on your report card," Mr. Mike says. "I'm proud of you."

He looks me in the eye and shakes my hand. I feel lucky that he's been there for me.

I pay for the paper, skate two blocks, and stop at the corner.

I pull out my phone, get on School View, and look at my grades again.

I have four C's and two B's.

They're the best grades I've had all year.

And I know they're going to get better.

AFTER SCHOOL. I enter the alley with Stan and Carl.

The tagging is gone. And we can ride our skateboards because there's no broken glass on the ground.

A cop car turns into the alley and pulls up next to us.

It's a young cop driving and an old one riding. They're the same cops who stopped Grady and me two months ago.

"A neighbor told us about you guys," the old cop says. "Thanks for what you're doing."

He reaches out and shakes our hands.

Dad would be proud of me.

RED CHURCH. We skate in the parking lot.

Stan and Carl do stair tricks down the back steps.

I stay on the ground and fall on my elbow doing kickflips.

I may not be a good skater. And I may fall a lot.

But I know how to get up.

ACKNOWLEDGMENTS

I would like to express my sincere gratitude to all of the people who gave me feedback while I was writing this book.

COFFEE HOUSE WRITERS GROUP: Paul Bello, Tracey Burke, Nicholas Chiazza, Sukie Fogg, Clyde Fugami, Anita Hamilton, Samantha Hancox-Li, Vuthy Hot, Steve Hovland, Alex Khansa, Melinda Lancaster, Darian Lane, Will Lee, Alex Lipinsky, John Lowell, Steve McCarthy, Janae Patino, Jean Pliska, Debby Putman, Amira Resnick, Patti Ann Searcy, Annick Tumolo, Henry Ward, Ron Wolff, AnneLise Wilhelmsen, Dennis Wolverton, Min, and Nick.

SOCIETY OF CHILDREN'S BOOK WRITERS
AND ILLUSTRATORS: Allison Aubin,
Heather Buchta, Tim Burke, Jonathan
Chew, Mandy Chew, Ernesto Cisneros,
Lisa Gold, Bryan Hilson, Chris
Jelbert, Wendy Loggia, Gretchen
McNeil, Q.L. Pearce, Bev Plass,
Kelly Powers, Jodi Rizzotto, Sara
Schonfeld, Alex Shane, Scott
Sussman, Esther Tenenbaum, Michaela
Whatnall, Sonja Wilbert.

SOUTHERN CALIFORNIA WRITERS
CONFERENCE: Laura Taylor, Cherie,
Janet, John, Jonathan, Justin, Lara,
Linda, and Marla.

WRITERS INK: Tim Burke, Emily
Heebner, Niki House, Teri Vitters,
and Eric Young.

Thank you, Pam Sheppard, for your
advice on creating this series.

Thank you, Laura Perkins, for your
feedback and careful editing.

Thank you, Betty-Jean, for your
patience, your feedback, your
suggestions, and for being my wife.

ABOUT THE AUTHOR

My dream of becoming a writer started at Whitworth University. I was lucky to have a teacher, Dr. Tammy Reid, who believed in me and encouraged me. After college, I began a career as an educator, teaching reading and English at a middle school. I went to college at night to earn a doctorate in education. I then served as a high-school principal and district administrator. One of the most important things I have learned is that every student can succeed. Set high goals, work hard, and never give up. Strive every day to achieve your dreams.

FINDING FORWARD BOOKS

At Finding Forward Books, we publish easy-to-read novels with positive life lessons that show teens overcoming challenges in their lives. Our goal is to help students improve their reading skills, increase their success in school, and gain hope.

The books are suitable for all students, including English Learners and those with learning disabilities. Lexile measures range from 390 to 560.

The books have been praised in *Kirkus Reviews*, *Publishers Weekly BookLife Reviews*, *Foreword Clarion Reviews*, and *BlueInk Reviews*.

ADDITIONAL TITLES

TAKEN AWAY. A teen learns to cope after his dad is sent to prison.

NO PLACE TO HIDE. A discouraged teen improves his reading skills.

NEVER WANTED. A neglected teen is placed in a foster home.

ALL ALONE. A teen learns to deal with his mom's alcoholism.

KNOCKED DOWN. A football player learns the importance of honesty.

TORN. A student with everything learns to care about another student who has nothing.

BLUE WALL. A troubled teen battles back from depression.

LETTERZ. A teen struggling with dyslexia learns how to succeed in school.

CANS. A teen who dreams of attending college struggles against poverty.

FINDING HOME. A homeless teen strives to build a better life for himself.

Finding Forward Books
Short Novels for Teens About
Issues Faced by Teens
www.findingforwardbooks.com